Alonzo's Emotions

by Merc & CaLisa

Alonzo has emotions just like you and me,
he's usually happy and smiling with glee.

But sometimes Alonzo
can get so annoyed,

like when he gets mad
if he's broken a toy.

And when he feels so irate
that he thinks he could faint

instead he makes art
with his colorful paint.

And sometimes Alonzo
can feel melancholy,

like when he wants tacos,
but is given tamales.

Instead of focusing
too long on food

he picks up his brush
to reset his mood.

Sometimes he feels nervous
and completely insane,

when he can't go outside
because of the rain.

Instead of just waiting,
trapped by the weather

he mixes his reds, blues,
and yellows together.

So when Alonzo feels bitter
or angry or stuck,
he funnels his feelings
into a paint brush.

He paints what he feels
and feels what he paints

until the canvas is covered
with all of his pains.

It's covered with happiness,
covered with tears,
covered with colors
that help calm his fears.

And when he feels done
he steps back and he sees
the beauty he made
and then he feels pleased.

Alonzo soothes his emotions
by painting his heart.

So if you're feeling down, go make some art!

Alonzo's Emotions was written by Merc Boyan.
Watercolor artworks by CaLisa Lee.

CAMP HEARTWOOD

books for kids

Camp Heartwood books are inspiring, creative, educational, and fun!
Our dream is to share wonder with the world.
We are in love with nature and art.

Want to see our books in your town?
Ask your local book store to add our books!
We'd love the help.

Made in the USA
San Bernardino, CA
16 August 2018